Dear Parent:
Your child's love of reading starts here!

Every child learns to read in a different way and at his or her own speed. Some go back and forth between reading levels and read favorite books again and again. Others read through each level in order. You can help your young reader improve and become more confident by encouraging his or her own interests and abilities. From books your child reads with you to the first books he or she reads alone, there are I Can Read Books for every stage of reading:

SHARED READING
Basic language, word repetition, and whimsical illustrations, ideal for sharing with your emergent reader

BEGINNING READING
Short sentences, familiar words, and simple concepts for children eager to read on their own

READING WITH HELP
Engaging stories, longer sentences, and language play for developing readers

READING ALONE
Complex plots, challenging vocabulary, and high-interest topics for the independent reader

ADVANCED READING
Short paragraphs, chapters, and exciting themes for the perfect bridge to chapter books

I Can Read Books have introduced children to the joy of reading since 1957. Featuring award-winning authors and illustrators and a fabulous cast of beloved characters, I Can Read Books set the standard for beginning readers.

A lifetime of discovery begins with the magical words "I Can Read!"

Visit www.icanread.com for information
on enriching your child's reading experience.

For Margaret, who is ALWAYS for the birds!
—H. P.

For Greg Sheldon
—L. A.

Gouache and black pencil were used to prepare the full-color art.

I Can Read Book® is a trademark of HarperCollins Publishers.

Amelia Bedelia is a registered trademark of Peppermint Partners, LLC.

Amelia Bedelia Is for the Birds. Text copyright © 2015 by Herman S. Parish III. Illustrations copyright © 2015 by Lynne Avril. All rights reserved. No part of this book may be used or reproduced in any manner whatsoever without written permission except in the case of brief quotations embodied in critical articles and reviews. Manufactured in China. For information address HarperCollins Children's Books, a division of HarperCollins Publishers, 195 Broadway, New York, NY 10007.
www.icanread.com

Library of Congress Cataloging-in-Publication Data

Parish, Herman.

Amelia Bedelia is for the birds / by Herman Parish ; pictures by Lynne Avril.

    pages cm.—(I can read. Level 1-beginning reading)

"Greenwillow Books."

Summary: Amelia Bedelia's after-school routine includes playing on her swing set every day, but when she discovers that robins are building a nest atop her slide, she watches them raise a family, instead.

ISBN 978-0-06-233425-1 (hardback)—ISBN 978-0-06-233424-4 (pbk.)

[1. Robins—Fiction. 2. Birds—Nests—Fiction. 3. Humorous stories.] I. Avril, Lynne, date. II. Title.

PZ7.P2185Aop 2015 [E]—dc23 2014025647

15 16 17 18 19 SCP 10 9 8 7 6 5 4 3 2 1 First Edition

Greenwillow Books

I Can Read!™

BEGINNING
1
READING

Amelia Bedelia
·Is for the Birds·

by Herman Parish ❀ pictures by Lynne Avril

Greenwillow Books, *An Imprint of* HarperCollins*Publishers*

Amelia Bedelia loved her swing set.

She had loved it when she was a baby

and she still loved it

now that she was big.

Every day when Amelia Bedelia
got home from school,
she raced outside and hopped on her swing.
She swung back and forth fifty times.

Then she slid down the slide five times.

After that she ran inside for a snack

and did her homework.

This was Amelia Bedelia's routine,

and it made her happy.

One afternoon, Amelia Bedelia

found a pile of sticks and leaves and grass

on the top of her slide.

"Yuck!" she said as she swept

everything onto the ground.

"Who made this mess on my slide?"

8

She slid down the slide superfast

and raced across the yard.

Some birds began chirping loudly

and fluttering around her head.

They were not singing a happy song.

Amelia Bedelia had a feeling

the birds were mad at her.

Amelia Bedelia ran into the kitchen.

"Look, Mom," she said,

pointing out the window.

"Those birds are making

a mess on my slide."

They watched the birds pile
more twigs and leaves and grass
on the top of the slide.

"Oh, how sweet,"
said Amelia Bedelia's mother.
"The robins are building a nest
on your slide."

"They can't do that,"
said Amelia Bedelia.
"I use my slide every day."

"Well, I guess you could
scare them away," said her mother.
"Or you could let them build a nest
and start a family."

"You mean there will be baby birds?"

asked Amelia Bedelia.

"Born in our backyard, on my slide?"

She gobbled down her snack.

"I'm going to the yard, Mom!" she said.

"Halt, young lady," said her mother.

"Your homework comes first."

After homework, dinner, and the dishes, Amelia Bedelia finally went back outside. She felt really bad about wrecking the bird nest.

She gathered more twigs and leaves and grass to replace what she had tossed away.

She got yarn, scraps of felt, and fluffy feathers from her arts-and-crafts box.

She left little heaps
of stuff at the bottom
of her slide.

"Here you go, Mr. and Mrs. Robin!"
she called to the birds.

"Here is a nest supply shop just for you!"

The next day

Amelia Bedelia woke up early.

Birds were chirping and singing

right outside her window.

They had been up for hours,

working away.

"Wow," said Amelia Bedelia at breakfast.

"Look at their new nest!"

"It reminds me of one
of your art projects, sweetie,"
said her mother, smiling.

"Try these binoculars,"
said her father.

"They will make your bird's-eye view
even better."

The mother robin sat on the nest
day and night, in rain and shine.
She sat there for almost two weeks.

One day Amelia Bedelia

saw something new.

"Mom!" she said.

"There are four tiny blue eggs!"

"They are robin's egg blue,"

said her mother.

"Of course they are,"

said Amelia Bedelia.

"What other color would they be?"

Finally, one day after school,

Amelia Bedelia spotted the mother bird

holding a worm in her beak.

Her babies were peeping.

"Feed me, feed me, feed me, feed me!"

The eggs had hatched!

At dinner that night

Amelia Bedelia's father talked about

a mess he had fixed at his job.

"Hey, Dad," said Amelia Bedelia.

"The next time someone at work

opens a can of worms,

bring some home for the robins."

The robin family gave Amelia Bedelia

a new routine.

She watched them

every morning before school

and every afternoon when she got home.

She saw the baby birds
get bigger.

She watched
their feathers grow.

She saw them
leave the nest
for the first time.

One day she watched them fly away.

Amelia Bedelia was so sad!

"When you grow up,

you will spread your wings

and fly away too," said her father.

"We'll have an empty nest,

just like Mr. and Mrs. Robin."

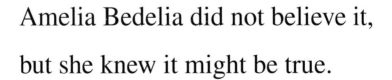

Amelia Bedelia did not believe it,
but she knew it might be true.

Now Amelia Bedelia's mom's eyes
were all watery,
the way they were when she watched
her favorite movies.
"That's a long way off, sweetie,"
her mom said.

29

Amelia Bedelia waited a few days
to make sure the robins were really gone.
Then she climbed up her slide
and carefully took the nest down.

Amelia Bedelia took the nest

to school to show her class.

She told them about

the robin family.

"That's amazing!" said Miss Edwards,

Amelia Bedelia's teacher.

"How did you find out

so much about robins?"

chirp! *chirp!*

chirp! *chirp!*

chirp! *chirp!*

"A little birdie told me,"

said Amelia Bedelia.